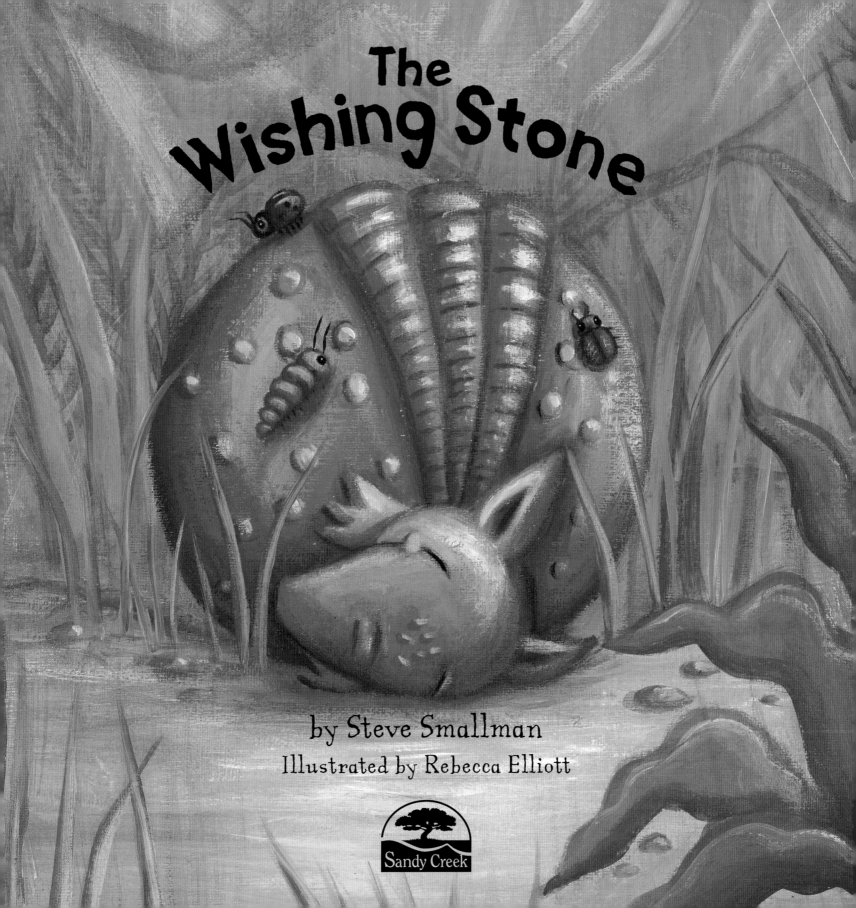

The Wishing Stone

by Steve Smallman

Illustrated by Rebecca Elliott

Sandy Creek

Armadillo lived in the swamp.

He was lonely and wished that he could find a friend.

But whenever anyone came near him,
he would roll himself up into a ball
and keep very still until they went away.

"What should we play today," squeaked Mouse. "Hide-and-seek?"

"No, I always lose," grumbled Flamingo.

"I know... **WATER FIGHT!**" shouted Monkey, and he pushed Flamingo into the swamp and jumped in after her.

Mouse couldn't swim, so he sat down
grumpily on a funny-looking stone.

"I wish I had a wading pool so
I could play, too," he said quietly.

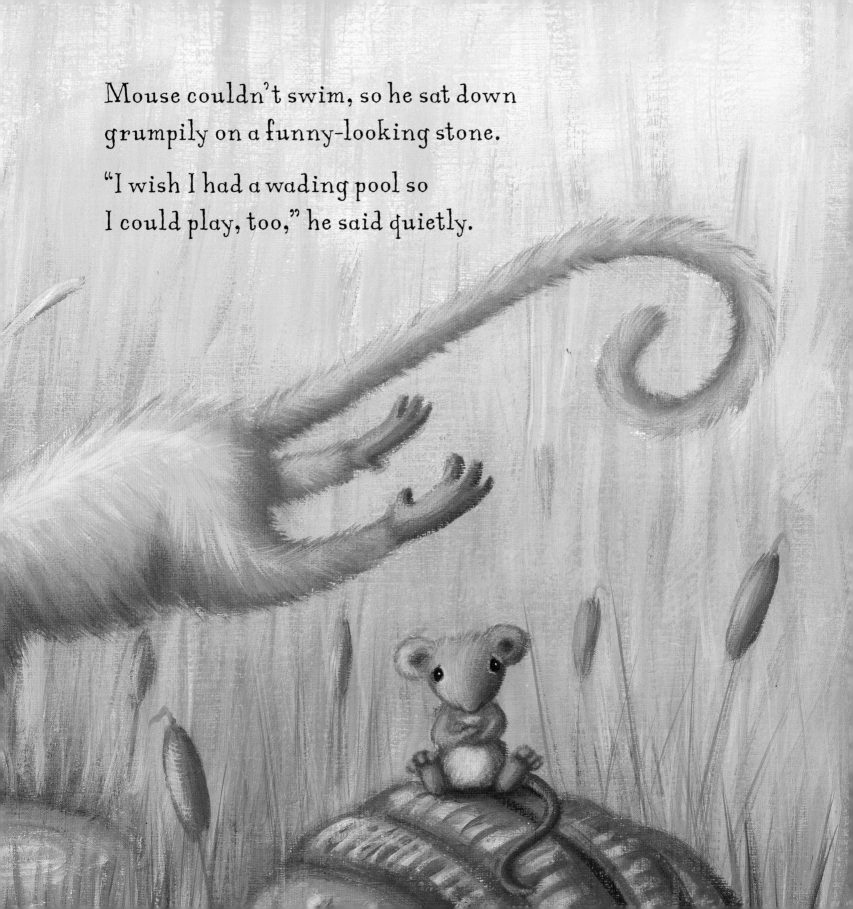

That night, Armadillo
got to work.

Using his strong claws,
he dug a wide hole and
filled it with water.

Then, tired out, he rolled up
into a ball and went to sleep.

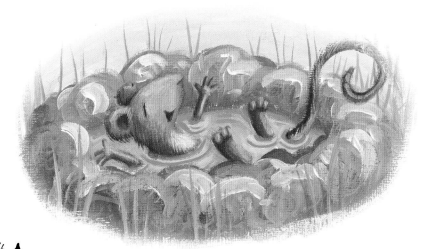

"A wading pool!" squeaked
Mouse excitedly the next morning.
"My wish came true.
That stone must be magic!"

"Let me try," said Flamingo, sitting on the stone. "I wish we had a secret den," she said.

"You'll have to wait until tomorrow for it to work," said Mouse.

That night, Armadillo
worked hard.

He cut down branches and
gathered leaves, and by the time
the sun started to rise, he had
made a wonderful secret den.

Tired out, he rolled up into
a ball and went to sleep.

"The wishing stone worked!"
squawked Flamingo the next day,
climbing inside the secret den.

"My turn!" cried Monkey,
sitting on the stone. "I wish there
was some food in here!"

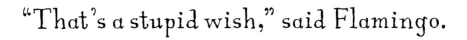

"That's a stupid wish," said Flamingo.

"Not if you're hungry," said Monkey.

"But you'll have to wait until tomorrow for it to work," said Mouse.

Armadillo liked to eat bugs.

So that night, he dug a hole inside the den, lined it with leaves, and then filled it with all the tastiest-looking bugs he could find.

Then, tired out, he rolled up
into a ball and went to sleep.

"Yuck!" Monkey, Flamingo, and Mouse didn't like bugs.

"That wishing stone is useless!" shouted Monkey, and kicked it toward the deepest part of the swamp.

"The wishing stone talks," gasped Mouse.
"And it can't swim!"

Monkey found a big stick and pushed it
into the water.

Armadillo grabbed it, and the three friends
pulled with all their strength until...

PLOP!

Out came Armadillo, soggy and gasping for breath.

"Did you make my wading pool?" asked Mouse.

"And our den?" added Flamingo. Armadillo nodded.

"What about the bugs?" asked Monkey.

"They're my favorite," sniffed Armadillo.
"I thought you would like them, too."

"Thank you. You're very kind," they replied, smiling.

Mouse, Flamingo, Monkey, and Armadillo
soon became best friends.

With Monkey's help, Armadillo learned to swim.
He even let Mouse ride on his back
in the deep end.

"Maybe wishes do come true,"
Armadillo thought happily.

Copyright © QEB Publishing, Inc. 2010

Published in the United States by
QEB Publishing, Inc.

This 2011 edition published by Sandy Creek by
arrangement with QEB Publishing, Inc.

ISBN 978-1-4351-3080-7

Printed in China
Manufactured December 2010

Editor: Amanda Askew
Designers: Vida and Luke Kelly

Sandy Creek
122 Fifth Avenue
New York, NY 10011

Lot 10 9 8 7 6 5 4 3 2 1

A CIP record for this book is available from the
Library of Congress.